W9-AXB-831

MARC BROWN

ARTHUR'S LOST PUPPY

LOST and FOUND

A Sticker Book

Random House 🏠 New York

Based on a teleplay by JOE FALLON

Copyright © 2000 by Marc Brown. All rights reserved under International and Pan-American Copyright
Conventions. Published in the United States by Random House Children's Books, a division of Random House,
Inc., New York, and simultaneously in Canada by Random House of Canada Limited, Toronto.
www.stepintoreading.com
Educators and librarians, for a variety of teaching tools, visit us at www.randomhouse.com/teachers
Library of Congress Cataloging-in-Publication Data
Brown, Marc Tolon.
Arthur's lost puppy / Marc Brown. p. cm. (Step into reading. A step 3 sticker book)
SUMMARY: Arthur and D.W. do not know what is wrong with Baby Kate
when they take her to the neighborhood fair—but Pal the puppy does.
ISBN 0-679-88466-1 (trade) — ISBN 0-679-98466-6 (lib. bdg.)
[1. Aardvark—Fiction.   2. Dogs—Fiction.   3. Babies—Fiction.   4. Fairs—Fiction.]
I. Title.   II. Series: Step into reading sticker books. Step 3. PZ7.B81618 Aqc   2003   [E]—dc21   2002013772
Printed in the United States of America   16 15 14 13 12 11 10 9 8 7
STEP INTO READING, RANDOM HOUSE, and the Random House colophon are registered trademarks of
Random House, Inc. ARTHUR is a registered trademark of Marc Brown.

Arthur and D.W. took Baby Kate
to the street fair.
Pal came along too.

There was lots to do.
Arthur gave Kate a ride
in a little fire truck
that went around and around.

D.W. got her face painted.

"Look, Kate!" she said.

"I'm a cat!"

But Kate was looking

at something else.

Suddenly, Kate began to cry.

"Are you hungry?" asked Arthur.

"Here's your bottle."

But Kate did not want her bottle.

"Wah! Wah! Wah!" she cried.

"Do you have a wet diaper?"
asked D.W.
But Kate's diaper was dry.
And still she cried.
"Wah! Wah! Wah!"

Arthur lifted the baby
from her stroller.

He rocked her
in his arms.

He tickled her tummy.

He made funny faces.

But still she cried.
"Wah! Wah! Wah!"

"Kate loves ice cream,"
said Arthur.
"Run to the store, D.W.,
and get her a cone."

D.W. tied Pal's leash to a bench
and went into the store.
A clown with balloons
walked by.
Pal barked at him.
"Woof! Woof! Woof!"

NO
DOGS
ALLOWED

When D.W. came out of the store,

Pal was gone!

She looked up and down the street.

"That dog is trouble!" she cried,

and she ran to tell Arthur.

"Oh, no!" cried Arthur.

"Why would Pal run away?"

"Maybe he's mad at you," said D.W.

"You yelled at him today

for chewing your slippers."

Arthur said nothing.

He just looked very sad.

But Kate had a lot to say.

"Wah! Wah! Wah!" she cried.

Then Arthur said,

"D.W., take Kate home.

Maybe she needs a doctor.

And I need to find Pal."

He began calling,

"Here, Pal! Here, Pal!"

Arthur passed the ring-toss table,
the bob-for-apples table,
and a table with pumpkin pies,
chocolate cakes, and cookies.

He wished there was a table
with hamburgers.
Pal would be sure to be
hanging around it!

"Have you seen a lost puppy?"
Arthur asked a police officer.
"A lost puppy?" said the officer.
"Yes, one was taken to the school."
"Oh, thank you!" said Arthur,
and he ran to the school.

But the lost puppy was not Pal.

Arthur sadly walked home.

Back at the street fair,
the clown with the balloons
tripped over his big floppy shoes.
CRASH! Down he went.
And as he fell, he let go
of his balloons.

Then guess what?

A little brown puppy jumped up

and grabbed the balloon strings

with his teeth.

The balloons rose
higher and higher.
Over the roofs, over the trees,
up, up, up they went.
And so did Pal!
"Look!" someone shouted.
"A flying puppy!"

Then suddenly—

BANG! POP! BANG!

The balloons hit a tall tree.

One by one they burst.

Pal floated slowly down.

When he got home,

he still had one

beautiful red balloon.

And one was all he needed
to make Baby Kate very happy.